To Tempt a Husband

After I Do

Lindsay Evans

Red Hills Publishing

For my readers.

Thank you.

Also by Lindsay Evans

Novels Available Now

Affair of Pleasure

Bare Pleasures (Miami Strong)

The CEO's Dilemma

A Delicate Affair

On-Air Passion (The Clarks of Atlanta)

Pleasure Under the Sun

Snowy Mountain Nights

Sultry Pleasure: A Billionaire Romance

The Pleasure of His Company (Miami Strong)

Untamed Love

The Wrong Fiancé

Professional Lovers Series

Seducing the Stripper (Professional Lovers Series Book 1)

Novella Anthology

Dim the Lights

Newsletter Sign-up

To keep up with the latest releases and get free reads, subscribe to my newsletter here: https://bit.ly/LindsayEvans

To Tempt a Husband

Chapter 1

Sylvie

"While I'm very flattered by your offer, Beau, I'm not interested in being your mistress," Sylvie said into her cell phone. "Or making you my side piece."

Finally in her house and out of the Atlanta summer heat, she slammed the front door shut behind her and kicked off her blood-red four-inch heels.

She dropped down to her real height of five feet five inches with a sigh of relief. Looking invincible was sometimes painful. With one hand still holding the phone to her ear, she rubbed the toes of one foot while balanced like a stork in her living room. She was only half-paying attention to the man trying to feed her gold-plated bullshit through the phone.

Her husband, Jason, had left a message while she was in a meeting and she was eager to call him back.

Sylvie tried to keep the impatience from her voice as she talked to Beau. When Jason called, she'd been working through the terms of a new supplier contract with her attorney. Since then, she'd been moving non-stop. With her Honda Civic pulled under the carport, she'd been about to check her voicemail when Beau called.

Her keys clattered in the ceramic dish by the door, her briefcase landed in its place on the roll top desk in the wide hallway, and she shrugged off her blazer. Feeling lighter and more comfortable, she walked deeper into the house wearing thin summer jeans and a cream silk blouse. The AC raised goosebumps over her sweat-dampened skin and the wisps of hair loosened from her French twist brushed her cheeks.

Damn Atlanta heat.

Sylvie moved quickly down the hallway, intent on getting to her favorite place in the house despite the phone call's interruption of her late Friday afternoon. Dammit, she should've listened to her first instinct and not answered the call. Too late now.

On the other end of the line, Beaumont Reddick, a potential business partner and a man who'd been shameless about pursuing her for the past few months, continued to plead his case.

"Don't dismiss my idea out of hand, Sylvie. I make a great partner in business, and in bed." The sounds of a low-voiced conversation came through the phone. "Anyway, think about it. I still plan to be at the meeting on Monday morning if you want to discuss it further."

There was absolutely nothing to discuss, so Sylvie made a noncommittal sound. Some men would just barrel on with their own assumptions regardless of what someone else told them. Particularly if that someone else was a woman. "See you at the meeting, Beau." She hung up.

Beau was pushy as hell, but he was going to soon learn Sylvie wasn't one of those people he could bulldoze over. Repeatedly, she'd made clear to him she wasn't in the market for a man. She already had one of those.

Distracted and annoyed by the phone call, she opened the French doors leading to the covered back porch. Then stopped dead, nearly all the air exploding from her lungs.

What in the fresh hell?

The man she expected to be on an African island thousands of miles away sat in one of the padded chairs facing the backyard. And Sylvie's sister, Michaela, was trying to sit in his lap.

"I'm so glad you're back," her sister said to Jason as she flashed her thick thighs in high-waisted sailor shorts. Michaela, gorgeous and in lucky possession of a body like an Instagram model, was on the verge of plopping her curvaceous ass on top of Jason's dick.

Was this a mirage?

No. A mirage was something a person *wanted* to see. There was absolutely no part of Sylvie interested in seeing her younger sister try to mount her husband while she watched.

Jealousy twisted in Sylvie's stomach, but she kept it cool and didn't rush across the suddenly too-big space and drag her sister off Jason by the hair. Barely.

"*Michaela*," Jason rumbled in warning. Sylvie hadn't made a sound but he glanced directly at her over her sister's shoulder.

After flashing her an apologetic look, he gripped Michaela's waist and held her up, preventing her from actually sitting on him. Sylvie supposed she should be grateful for small mercies.

"Good afternoon, Jason." She paused in the doorway, hand tightly squeezing her cell phone. "I was just about to listen to your voicemail message." She smiled tightly at her sister. "Michaela."

"Oh. Hey, Sylvie." Michaela jackrabbited from Jason's restraining hold but didn't have the decency to look embarrassed. If anything, she seemed smug. Like she had every right to touch him. "I thought you were still at work."

"I thought you had your own house." Sylvie showed her teeth.

"Oh my God, stop it already." Her brat setting on high, Michaela rolled her eyes. "Mama and Daddy left this house to us both, not just to you."

"Maybe so, but Jason doesn't come with your share of the property," Sylvie said, striving for calm. As usual, her sister was trying her patience. Weren't siblings supposed to get over stupid rivalry by their age?

Not that Michaela was her rival for anything, or anyone. Michaela had established herself as the winner of whatever one-sided competition they had a long time ago. Considered the more beautiful Barrington sister, she'd always gotten her way when their parents were alive. More than one of Sylvie's boyfriends had *somehow* ended up in her bed. And when she met one of Sylvie's potential investors—a much older Atlanta millionaire—Michaela quickly dated and married him. They split less than a year ago, leaving her with half the millionaire's money and twin toddlers.

No. Whenever Michaela set herself up to win, Sylvie was usually better off just getting out of her way.

Except... If Michaela thought she was about to snatch up Sylvie's man, she was out of her damn mind.

Jason. The pulse knocked hard in her throat as she looked at him. Despite the heat, he wore a dress shirt with the sleeves rolled up to the elbows. The gray pinstripe slacks fit his slim hips well, the black belt around his waist inviting her eyes to stare at the heavy-looking bulge behind his zipper. Sylvie swallowed. When she yanked her eyes from Jason's crotch, she tumbled into his gaze. The invitation in his eyes pulled Sylvie closer. She'd taken a step toward him before she could guard herself against his powerful effect on her.

He stood up. And up. Sylvie blinked in surprise. Had he grown bigger and more imposing since the last time she saw him in Tarbemi a year ago?

She drank in his cedar brown skin, wide shoulders, and the sinfully sensual lips framed by a neatly trimmed goatee.

While Jason had always been handsome, in her mind, he remained young. A full five years younger than her and forever the somewhat naïve twenty-four-year-old who'd suggested an outrageous marriage scheme she'd agreed to out of frustration and fear. The man in front of her now looked not at all juvenile.

Sexy, yes.

Commanding, absolutely.

Young? Not so much anymore. The proof was in the way her body responded to him.

"Michaela, watching you being rude to Sylvie isn't how I plan to spend any of my time here." The rumbling bass in Jason's voice touched something in Sylvie, unexpectedly making her shiver. "If you don't mind, I need some privacy to speak with *my wife*." His particular emphasis on the last two words brought Sylvie's eyebrows flying up.

Was he just claiming her as his wife to make Michaela jealous? It had been a while since Jason and Michaela were together, but maybe seeing her sister again—the fun Barrington sibling who was once again available since her recent divorce—made him realize how much he missed her and wanted her back. Sylvie swallowed her unease and tried to keep her face blank.

Michaela meanwhile cocked a flirtatious hip, her pretty smile creasing her cheeks in a way that made her look innocent and sweet. "Come on, Jason. You just got here. I thought we'd grab a drink together since you haven't been here in so long."

Sylvie knew very well the last time Jason had been in this house. It was the day he asked her to marry him five years ago. The same day Michaela dumped him.

"Go on home, Michaela. My husband and I need to have a chat." Sylvie crossed the porch and sank down into the chair Jason just abandoned. She had a feeling whatever he wanted to talk about, she needed to be sitting down for it.

Her sister pouted as if to say she had him first. One look at Jason's face, though, and whatever she saw there must have convinced her that now was *not* the time for her foolishness.

"Fine. We'll talk later." With an exaggerated roll of her hips, Michaela went through the French doors and disappeared inside. "Bye now, y'all." Her voice floated back out to the porch like a siren's call aimed at Jason alone.

Bitch.

No. Her sister wasn't a bitch. Just entirely too used to getting what she wanted. Sylvie mentally begged her dead parents' forgiveness for calling her that, even if it was only in her mind.

"That was definitely not the welcome back to Atlanta I had in mind." Jason, hands in the pockets of his pinstripe gray slacks, turned from the door where Michaela disappeared. A smile curved his lips. His dark eyes rested on Sylvie's with the warmth she had become achingly familiar with.

Now that her sister was gone and not messing with her equilibrium, she jumped up from the chair. This was *Jason*. No matter how suddenly taller and finer he was, this was the man she'd been chatting with nearly every day for the last five years. The same man who helped to save her business when she was at her wit's end.

"It's good to see you." She stepped into his arms, something she'd begun to naturally do as their friendship deepened.

"I couldn't tell by that full-on glare you gave me," he said with laughter threaded through his voice.

Jason's arms slid around her, hard and warm, the muscles of his chest firm against her breasts. He smelled fresh and clean, the mint-infused cologne he wore woven with his own sun-warmed masculine scent and sweat. The solid heat of him sank into her body and made every part of her take notice. Her nipples tingled and grew hard. The space between her legs moistened and a hot blush scalded her cheeks.

Oh, God. Did he notice?

Desperately turned on but trying not to show it, Sylvie pulled her arms from around Jason's neck. She cleared her throat. Without comment, he released her, those eyes still watching her with an unfamiliar intensity, devouring her in a way she'd never experienced before.

"What are you doing in Georgia? You never come to America anymore. And, if my calendar isn't wrong, we're not supposed to meet in Tarbemi until August." It was only mid-June.

"I thought about waiting," Jason said. He slid his hands back into his pockets and took a few steps of his own back. "However, what I need to say to you can't wait."

Her stomach clenched with sudden worry. "Is something wrong?"

It didn't look like it. Over the years, Sylvie had come to know her husband more than a little. He didn't look upset, just intense in a way she was used to seeing when he talked about business.

"No, there's nothing wrong. At least, I hope there isn't. Though it depends on your reaction."

"What are you talking about, Jason?" Impatience snapped at Sylvie. She crossed her arms tightly over her chest, trying to subdue the worry agitating behind her breastbone. "Stop freaking me out and get to the point, please."

His lips tightened briefly. "I need an heir, Sylvie. I'm here to ask you to have my baby."

Chapter 2

Jason

Jason was glad he'd been sitting down when Sylvie came out to the back porch. She looked...incredible. Only a hint of make-up touched her fine-boned face, allowing her natural beauty that had only grown over the years to shine through. Her skin, a shade or two lighter than his, glowed with health and perspiration. From her French-pedicured toes to the elegant twist of her straightened hair, she was everything he'd longed for since he gave up sex with other women two years ago.

How had he ever fooled himself into thinking he'd only ever want her as a friend?

Eyes wide, she stood in front of him with her crossed arms plumping up her small breasts under the silk blouse. A breeze from the overhead fan rippled the silk over her skin, making it impossible to miss how her nipples, hard points of temptation he burned to explore with his mouth and hands, pressed against the fabric. Arousal fisted in his belly.

"What did you just say?" Sylvie stared at him.

Okay, so it wasn't like he'd expected her to jump for joy with the idea of having his baby, but this shock was dampening. Or dick softening, in his case. He'd come to Atlanta hoping she was open to the idea. But she looked shocked, like he was there to kill her puppy and its whole family.

"Let's go to your office and talk about this," he suggested. "It might be a little better."

"But—"

He took her elbow before she could protest again and led her inside the house toward her office. At the last minute, he changed his mind and headed toward the kitchen instead. There, he guided her to a stool at the kitchen island and went to find some of the iced tea she always kept in the fridge.

He poured them both a glass but diluted his with more water and lemon. Once she was relaxed on the barstool with half the glass of ice tea in her, he brought it up again.

"Have you seriously never thought about having children?"

"With the way our marriage began, I actually never did." A faint frown wrinkled her forehead. "Maybe I should have." Her glass clicked on the counter when she put it down. The frown deepened. "That wasn't part of our initial agreement, though."

True enough.

They'd married when he was twenty-four and she was thirty. He'd needed a wife to inherit his grandmother's company and fortune, and Sylvie had been desperate for any fresh ideas to get her family business out of the red. Later, she'd even confessed to feeling guilty about the way Michaela had ended things with him.

From what he remembered, her business had meant more to her than anything else. Especially at the time they agreed to the marriage.

With everything they'd already been through together, that afternoon felt like a lifetime ago...

Chapter 3

Jason

Five Years Ago

Jason knocked on Michaela's bedroom door, the strap of his backpack digging into his shoulder with a feeling of anticipation. The door flew open and Michaela dragged him inside.

"Congrat—!" He began but she slammed her mouth over his and started to pull off his clothes, fingers nimbly unbuttoning his jeans and working their way inside. Laughing, he pulled back. "Stop, Michaela. Your sister is downstairs."

"So what? After two years together, she knows we're having sex." She grabbed his dick, tugging on it to get him hard.

At twenty-four, it didn't take much for him to fatten up in her hands, not to mention her touch felt good as fuck. But he pulled back. *Sylvie* was in the house. Michaela's older sister had always been kind to him, talked with him and fed him whenever Michaela was running late. She wasn't as pretty as Michaela but had a quiet strength and constancy which reminded him of the patron goddess, Isidima, of his African island home.

He'd never disrespect Sylvie by having sex in the house while she was around. Even if it was a celebratory fuck for Michaela's good news. She'd gotten the prestigious fellowship she applied for and had shrieked the news in Jason's ear over the phone. Which was why he was there with champagne to celebrate.

But apparently, she wanted to toast her good news with his dick.

"It's one thing for Sylvie to know and another to hear us." Michaela was a screamer. Great for his ego, bad for anybody within a half-mile radius. "You should've just come to my place if you were in the mood for sex." He gave her a quick kiss before carefully prying his dick out of her hands. Jason shrugged off his backpack and dropped it by the closed door.

"You know I'm *always* in the mood for sex." She tried to follow him across the room but he put her rolling desk chair between them.

"Let's go out and celebrate," Jason said. "Dinner. Ice cream. Whatever you want. This is a big deal."

After another few unsuccessful minutes trying to get him naked, she flopped backward on her bed. "I can't believe you're serious about this. Sylvie doesn't care. She's probably out there counting her hundred-dollar bills or something. Since mom and dad left her the shop, she doesn't care about anything else. Not even the boyfriend she's supposed to have."

It was the first thing Jason was hearing about Sylvie having a boyfriend. Not that it mattered.

"So you want to go out and play cookie monster, or what?" Michaela was crazy about those giant cookie cakes they sold at the mall. For her, paradise was a pint of vanilla bean ice cream on top of one of those monstrosities.

She pouted. "I don't feel like it."

"Okay." He reached for his backpack. "Then we can just celebrate here."

She perked up.

"No sex." The backpack was heavy and cold in his lap.

Michaela perked back down. Her lower lip poked out again. "Come on! Stop being so boring."

A challenge like that from her usually got him going. But he was nearly twenty-five now and learning he didn't have to pick up every dare she threw down. Despite being a couple of years older than her, he'd admittedly been easy to manipulate. He'd allowed it, figured it wouldn't do any harm.

They'd met at Harvard while he was getting his MBA and she was dabbling in astrophysics as a first-year graduate student, a bored genius. Aside from his grandmother, she was the smartest person he'd ever met and he immediately set out to get her under him. An illicit library fuck, the first time they hooked up, turned into a now two-year relationship. A few months ago, she'd agreed to marry him when he told her the inheritance conditions he had hanging over his head. They were still having fun and she'd said, "why not?"

Lately though, Jason started to question whether or not they were still having fun.

"Come back to my place with me and we can celebrate for the rest of the day and night," he said, and she knew he was good for it, too. His stamina even impressed him sometimes.

"That's too far." With her back against the headboard, Michaela sat with her arms wrapped around her bent legs. She rested her chin on top of her knees. "I guess this is for the best since I have something to tell you anyway."

"What's on your mind?"

"I want to break up."

For a second, he was sure he'd had an auditory hallucination. Because there was no way she said…

"Where is this coming from?"

"Are you hearing yourself right now?" She sat back, leveling a frown at him. "Any real boyfriend who actually gives a shit would be asking other questions. Why? What did I do? How can I fix this? But not you. That's why I'm breaking up with you. You, Jason Fallou, have the emotional depth of a Petri dish."

"Only five seconds ago, you were trying to fuck." He was confused as hell right now.

"You also have an amazing stroke game to go with your big dick. You can't blame me for trying to get it in one more time."

Shock pushed Jason to his feet, dropping the backpack off his lap and to the bed. He spun around in Michaela's room, unable to get his bearings. "Michaela, we agreed to get married. I told you why."

"Even though I agreed to it before, now it's not enough." She shrugged. "Sorry."

Jason's ears rung like a struck bell. He hadn't been in America long, only the last five years, on and off, to get his degrees. Now, with Michaela staring at him cold-eyed from her bed, he truly felt stranded in a foreign country, an unfamiliar place with mores and a culture he didn't understand. For years, he'd really thought she understood him, not just as a person, but as the businessman who needed her to marry him.

He'd never felt so wrong.

Because he wasn't someone who needed to be told to "get the fuck out" twice, he gave Michaela a brisk nod. "Okay. You've obviously made up your mind."

He grabbed his backpack and stumbled out of the room. Even after seeing the surprise flash across her face, he kept going. Soon, though, he stopped.

It was stress, he told himself, standing at the bottom of the stairs. He looked up to where he'd just come from. Maybe the surprise she'd shown meant she expected him to fight for their relationship.

Pulse thudding hopefully in his throat, Jason turned around and headed back up to Michaela's room.

They'd been a team for two years. Some things scared Michaela and made her want to run. Maybe with his twenty-fifth birthday coming in just a few weeks—the deadline for them to get married—Michaela was getting nervous. What the Americans called cold feet.

As much as he'd mastered being able to speak English with an American accent while living in Tarbemi for most of his life, there were just some American cultural things he'd missed out on. If he was going to be married to an American wife, he had to be aware of and understand the things related to their culture. With the straps of the backpack settled properly over both shoulders, he slowly walked down the hallway, thinking about what he'd have to say to ease his soon-to-be bride's mind.

"Yeah, he's gone." Jason heard Michaela's voice through her half-open door as he approached her room. "I know, right?" she said to whoever she was talking to. "I tried to get him to give me some before I broke it off. He totally clit blocked me."

Well, if sex was what she needed to feel more secure about their future, he could give in. Not in the house, though. Maybe in his car...?

For most of his adult life, Jason had concerned himself with the new responsibilities he would have once he took control of his grandmother's company. He'd learned the integral parts of running a business from his American schools. But hadn't thought to get ready to be a partner and a husband. Clearly a mistake. Michaela needed a man she could see as her husband, not just the boy she'd been having fun with at university.

Jason drew a breath. Yes, he'd shift some of his attention to learning his new role. Michaela deserved it. He lifted a hand to knock on her bedroom door.

"He is so much better of a fuck than Greg, and his dick is bigger, too. Last month, I was trying to show Greg what Jason does to make me squirt but this dude wasn't having it..."

Jason froze. Mentally, he re-played what Michaela just said, because she couldn't mean what he thought.

Greg. Last month.

His feet felt stuck to the wooden floor. He couldn't move. He could only listen to the words of the one-sided conversation while all his personal plans for the rest of his life crumbled to dust.

"You're right. I would be guaranteed good dick for the rest of our married life. But what if there's better out there and I just haven't had it yet?" A pause. "Girl... I think I'm just too young to get married. Yeah, I told him I would but I was dickmatized at the time. It was probably after a session with the head doctor. Jason's tongue is out of this world." Another silence. "Stop, don't make me regret breaking up with him. If only we could just keep it a casual girlfriend-boyfriend thing." The sound of Michaela blowing out a harsh breath and flopping down on the bed came through the door. "Fuck, I *do* feel a little bad about bailing on this marriage thing. Damn..."

Jason didn't realize he had walked away from the room until he felt the sun burning into his face and smelled overly sweet flowers and rich, dark earth.

Somehow, he'd made it to the back garden of the house and was kneeling in the middle of a flower bed. The backpack pressed cold and heavy against his thighs.

Michaela had fucked someone else. She talked openly to her friends about what they did in bed. Did she even believe what she said about his so-called "emotional depth"?

His thoughts came lightning fast, one after the other as they often did. But this was nothing like when he was working to solve a problem. This wasn't productive or helpful.

A harsh laugh spilled from his mouth. How long had she been fucking other guys and making him believe they still had a future as a couple?

Weeks ago, he'd graduated from business school, already making plans for the CEO position he would take on once he married and moved back to Tarbemi. He'd rented an apartment in Atlanta to be close to Michaela for the summer, respecting the home she shared with her sister.

He swallowed a bout of nausea. She'd taken him for a fool and he'd gone along for the ride. When Michaela told him she wanted to savor every last moment of her freedom until their wedding just days before his twenty-fifth birthday, he'd believed her. He had placed the future of his business and his inheritance in her hands.

He thought she at least respected him. The fuck she did.

Jason tore open the backpack and grabbed the champagne he'd brought over to celebrate Michaela's good news. It was still cold. Which was strange since it felt like hours had passed since he walked into her room and got his feet kicked out from under him.

The champagne cork popped. Jason grabbed the bottle by the neck and put it to his mouth. Cool liquid flowed over his tongue and he drank and drank and drank. The scent of the garden nearly made him sick when he was done. His mouth was wet with the taste of the champagne but he still couldn't make sense of what just happened.

The smell of the dirt was strong, his knees sinking into the red earth still damp from the previous day's rain.

Shit. He probably looked like a fool there on his knees, waiting to be saved when he needed to save himself. But how?

"Who's there?"

He jerked at the sound of the surprised voice. It was low and husky, nothing like Michaela's. A figure appeared around the cluster of tall pink flowers and he lurched to his feet, tumbling the champagne bottle to the dirt.

"Sylvie?" He blinked at her, focused on the woman whose garden he was probably about to throw up in. Her face, pretty in a subtle way, had a slightly pinched look. The end of her high ponytail brushed one shoulder and she wore some sort of wrap dress, pale yellow, that clung to her subtle curves.

When did he start noticing Sylvie's body? Jason blinked. It wasn't a good look for him to get drunk at her place. He should've driven back to his apartment. Less humiliating that way.

A frown touched Sylvie's forehead and her eyes went soft with concern. "Are you okay?" She came closer on bare feet, walking down the paved path into the small garden.

Her toenails were painted white, he noticed through his slowly fogging senses. It was a weekday and normally she'd be at work. No, she usually took Thursdays off, that's right. Then he realized he was staring.

"Sorry to disturb you," he said.

"You're not disturbing me at all." Her eyes swept over him and he was sure he looked a wreck with his dirty jeans and the half-finished bottle of champagne at his feet. "What's wrong?"

Not wanting to seem weak in front of her, he straightened his back and yanked his wandering thoughts about her dress and body back under control.

Just tell her nothing's wrong. Then you can get a cab home, sleep off the stupid champagne, then figure out what to do next.

"Michaela just dumped me." Jason frowned. That wasn't what he meant to say. He opened his mouth again to show the strength his grandmother had instilled in him. "She's fucking someone else."

Was he possessed? Why was he spilling his guts to this woman he'd always admired? The last thing he wanted was for Sylvie to think of him as some child who needed his scraped knees kissed and tended to.

Her face settled into sympathetic lines. "That's unexpected. I thought the two of you were eventually getting married."

"Until today, I thought so too."

She sucked in a surprised breath.

Then he spilled his guts about everything. Might as well since he was standing there hemorrhaging feelings. While the afternoon sun scorched him through his plain white T-shirt, he told her about his grandmother's will, the planned marriage to fulfill the terms of his inheritance, and the overheard conversation about Greg with the tiny dick.

Sylvie choked on something that sounded like a laugh. He must have said the thing about Greg and his micro dick out loud.

"Maybe Greg has some qualities that make up for his lack of size." Her lips pressed together and her eyes brightened with amusement.

That's cool. Someone else might as well find his situation funny.

"I'm sorry, Jason." She cleared her throat and the threat of laughter faded from her face. "At least your heart isn't broken, or it doesn't seem to be."

Through the liquor crowding out any lucid thoughts, he realized it was true. His heart felt fine. Only his pride was wounded. Not to mention his chance of inheriting was about to be fucked up the ass with a cactus.

"I'm sure you can still find someone to marry you," Sylvie said.

Why couldn't he stop blabbing his thoughts out loud? Oh, right. The fucking champagne. It fizzed his blood, made a mess of his cognitive abilities, and lowered his inhibitions all the way to the basement.

"Would *you* marry me?"

Sylvie's eyes widened, then she appeared to quietly consider him. "If you weren't my sister's boyfriend, yes. I would."

"I'm not Michaela's anything." The bench a short distance away caught his attention. If he didn't sit down soon, he was seriously going to fall over. "Come sit with me."

At the back of his mind, he knew under normal circumstances, he wouldn't have had the balls to put his hand on Sylvie. But the champagne made him bold. He took her elbow and gently towed her to the cement bench where he gratefully sat down with a sigh.

Jesus. It felt good to get off his feet. What was he talking about before? Oh, yes. Whose man he was or could be.

"So what can I give you in return for marrying me?" he asked.

Sylvie clasped her hands in her lap and was quiet for a long time. "You're smart. Michaela said once how you could solve all the world's problems with your big brain."

"And just what problem do you need my big *brain* to solve."

She clapped a hand over her mouth, but a shout of laughter escaped anyway. "Sorry. I must be turning into a twelve-year-old boy." Sylvie waved a hand at the bottle of champagne Jason realized he was still clutching like a pacifier. "Can I have some of that?"

"Sure." He passed it over and watched as she put the bottle to her lips and took a big swallow. Her mouth sealed over the top and her throat worked as she drank. His dick perked up, heat gathering in his balls as he imagined her sucking on *him* with equal thirst.

What the fuck?

Jason casually arranged his linked hands over his lap and cleared his throat. He looked anywhere but at Sylvie. At the gardens, the little green chest of tools lying half-open nearby. Shit, he even stared long and hard at a couple of bees diving deep into the pink heart of a flower. Nope. He shouldn't look at them either.

Damn. What the hell was wrong with him? He subtly adjusted himself and blew out a breath of air.

No more champagne for him. Ever.

"So, are you going to tell me what you need from me?" he croaked.

Maybe it was the champagne. Or the damn bees pollinating everything in sight. But at the end of the conversation, he and Sylvie agreed to marry. He'd get his inheritance and she'd have access to what he had in his head, and potentially some investment capital as well.

He still thought he was getting more out of the deal, but they'd promised each other to wait until the next day when he was sober and she was less...financially panicked to make the final decision on the marriage.

The following day, stone-cold sober, neither changed their minds.

Chapter 4

Sylvie

Have a *baby* with Jason?

Sylvie felt like someone had hit her upside the head with her grandmother's church purse. She sat on the stool at the kitchen island, her hands clasped around the cold glass of iced tea. A few feet away, Jason leaned against the counter, arms crossed over his chest, his face in its usual solemn lines.

She put the iced tea to her lips, drinking deeply from it to give herself more time. Finally, she put the glass down. Her nervous fingers flitted over to adjust the vase of pink azaleas she'd picked from the garden that morning.

"Tell me what you're thinking, Jason," she finally said. Because this desire for an heir didn't just come out of nowhere.

He shifted his hips against the counter, probably because of the drawer handle digging into his butt, and her eyes dropped below his belt buckle before she realized how inappropriate that was. Especially because of the way her core tightened and grew wet, imagining—

"When we agreed to marry, I wasn't thinking about children," Jason said, pulling her attention back where it belonged. "However, now I'm financially secure and would like a child to leave everything to when I'm gone."

His grave eyes held hers. "You and I are married. It makes sense we should have the child together."

He didn't mention anything about love, Sylvie thought with a hard swallow. Not that she had any business considering their relationship in a sentimental way. After all, this started as a bloodless bargain between two people who were only acquaintances.

Sylvie held the breath in her lungs and slowly let it out.

"You don't need *me* to have a baby," she said. "I'm sure any woman in Tarbemi would be happy to fall into your bed." On her yearly visits to the island kingdom, she'd seen how women looked at Jason. Their gazes on him were hungry, even when they'd been kind and welcoming to Sylvie.

He stirred against the counter, an overwhelming presence in the kitchen that usually seemed a little too big. "Are you saying you don't want to have children?"

Sylvie clasped her hands together on the countertop.

She and Jason had talked a lot over the years. He knew how she felt about children. They weren't a need. She could happily not have them. Despite being terrible at running a business, her parents had been deeply career-oriented. The time they'd spared for Sylvie and Michaela was the bare minimum. She was convinced if her parents had been able to afford a full-time nanny, then a stranger would've been the one to raise them.

Like her parents, Sylvie loved her work. But she didn't want to parent the way Lena and Lionel Barrington had.

"Don't put words in my mouth, Jason. I've actually never given much thought to becoming a mother. You know that. I don't call myself child-free, but I've also never day-dreamed about being pregnant either."

"From what I've heard and seen, it's not something many people *should* dream about." His face took on a look of exaggerated horror. The expression of a man who'd probably seen one too many birthing videos.

"And that's something you want to inflict on me?"

He flinched a little. "*Inflict.* What a word." But a smile lingered around his full mouth. His goatee looked soft enough to touch, highlighting firm and well-shaped lips Sylvie had imagined kissing far too many times. Jason was such a gorgeous man.

The image bloomed suddenly in her mind. A little girl with Jason's intelligence and warm brown skin. A boy laughing and adorable in his happiness, with a duplicate of Jason's single dimple flashing from his chubby cheek.

A shocked breath left Sylvie's lips and the image of those two phantom children loosened a swarm of butterflies in her stomach. She swallowed and looked down at her fingers gripped so tightly together that the tendons pushed out against her skin.

"Does the thought of making a baby with me turn you off so much?" Jason asked softly, his voice a low rumble in the kitchen.

The problem was it turned her all the way *on*, and if it wasn't for the curious look in his eyes, she'd think he was playing with her. What woman who liked men wouldn't slap her own ass and bend over for him? Heat blazed in Sylvie's face.

She took a breath. "Look, that's not the question."

"Then what is it?" Suddenly, he was too close, his body heat scorching through her clothes.

Sylvie spun the stool to face him, grounding herself with her arm still braced against the kitchen island. Dark eyes looked into hers, flicked down to her mouth. She caught her breath.

Jason's hair was just long enough on top for her to grip, and his mouth held a curve of such impossible seduction that heat pulsed between her legs. His eyes dove deeply into hers, probing and probably seeing far too much. Sylvie fought to control her breath and the arousal wetting her panties.

She *couldn't* have him.

They hadn't married for love, never shared a bed or bodily fluids, but over the five years, mutual respect and a cherished friendship had grown between them. She didn't want to lose that friendship. Not to something as fleeting as lust.

Sylvie had had lovers since they married. She knew Jason had, too. It was only in the last couple of years when she'd started to fall for him that she'd stopped sleeping with other men. It was hopeless to want Jason that way, so she'd never approached him with her desire.

It wasn't his fault she wished there was more between them.

"Jason..." All her longing, frustration, and regret poured out of her on the breath she spared to say his name.

Then, for the first time since their quick press of lips at their courthouse wedding, he kissed her.

Shocked, Sylvie drew in a quick breath. Which was a mistake because she accidentally inhaled him and drew his intoxicating essence inside her. Sylvie shivered. His mouth was light against hers, no physical or emotional pressure, just a gentle waiting.

He brushed his lips across hers. Once. Twice.

Her belly clenched tight at the fluttering sensations against the sensitive flesh of her mouth. This was how it could be between them, something inside her screamed. Desire ignited between her thighs and pushed aside any thoughts about the original terms of their marriage.

Moaning in surrender, she pushed her lips harder against his, taking what he offered.

"Fuck." He groaned against her mouth and the sound sank into her skin.

Jason kissed Sylvie raw and filthy and wet, and she kissed him right back. She licked into his mouth, whimpering with arousal as he sucked on her tongue, the slow suction like leisurely and endlessly sublime tugs on her clit. Her arms wound around his neck as he yanked her against him. Just that quickly, her nipples were hard and aching, and the trickle of wetness between her legs became a river.

She wanted to climb him like a stripper pole. Push him back on the kitchen island, rip off their clothes, and ride him until they both collapsed in a pool of cum and sweat. A moan of longing left her throat.

Sylvie wanted to make love to him.

She wanted to keep him in her life forever.

But that would never happen. With a hoarse cry, she pulled her mouth from Jason's. He stared at her in surprise, his lips wet from their kiss, eyes heavy with lust. Sylvie clenched her fists to stop herself from reaching for the hard dick poking her stomach. From dropping to her knees and slobbing it down like she'd been dreaming about for years. Her core spasmed and dripped.

Oh, God. She was losing her mind.

She stumbled back and smacked into the barstool, hitting it so hard it skidded across the kitchen floor.

"Easy." Only Jason's gentle hold on her shoulders kept her from pitching ass-first to the ground. "No need to hurt yourself over a kiss." Despite his soft words, the desire in his gaze threatened to catch her on fire.

She cleared her throat and more carefully stepped back and out of his arms. Part of her wanted to thank him for saving her from a humiliating fall, but mostly she blamed him for everything that just happened. Not for her near-fall but the irrefutable knowledge she now had of what he tasted like, how his hard dick felt pressed against her.

There was no going back to the way things were between them.

Warm. Friendly. Strictly defined.

Knowing this almost shattered her. "I—I have to go." Though she wasn't normally a coward, Sylvie ran out of the kitchen like her feet were on fire. The last thing she saw was Jason watching her with a look of concern, his dick pointing right at her through his slacks.

* * *

Later that night, Sylvie sat in her darkened bedroom, painfully aware of Jason in the guest room down the hall. After their kiss, she'd been too scared to stay home. She'd rushed through the house, grabbing up the things she'd left— purse, car keys, shoes—and jumped in the car. Her favorite café a few miles away was her haven and her escape. There, she silenced her phone, pulled up a novel on her e-reader, and immersed herself in a fantasy world until the café closed. It was well after dinner time when she crept back home and snuck into her room.

While she was out, she had a couple of missed calls from Beau but he would just have to wait until Monday morning.

Michaela had also texted, all a bunch of random messages about Jason. What was he doing now? Did Sylvie care if Michaela took him out to a club tonight? How had he gotten so much hotter in the last five years?

Just call him and ask, Sylvie finally responded, trying not to let her frustration and growing anger show.

Michaela: *I don't have his new number. Got lucky and found out he was going to be in Atlanta because of social media. Give me his #?*

Sylvie didn't answer after that.

She was running from her own feelings. Again. It was safer than confronting her jealousy of Michaela, or the desire Jason effort-lessly sparked inside her. A shuddering sigh left her lips. One touch from him and it felt like an earthquake rumbled through her body and her life, disrupting everything that existed before.

The close friendship she and Jason had built.

The lie she'd told herself that she didn't want anything more.

Fresh from the shower, she sat in the cushioned window seat overlooking the garden where Jason had proposed to her. The A/C blew cool air into the room, making her shiver in her oversized sleep shirt. Goosebumps rippled over her skin and she hugged her knees to her chest. In the garden, pink and white summer flowers glowed under the moonlight as five-year-old memories began to overwhelm her.

She'd come from a meeting with her business accountant, reeling from bad news. If they didn't turn the shop around within the next six months, they wouldn't be able to afford their rent or two remaining employees. A mix of dread and resignation distracted her as she walked into the garden. At that moment, she'd desperately craved *something* to take her mind off the burden her life had become. The endless cycle of needing money to keep Barrington Beauty afloat, pay taxes on her parents' house, and help Michaela with her graduate school living expenses.

Sylvie heard a noise. She called out and turned a corner. A man knelt in the dirt, gripping an open bottle of champagne. His thighs were spread wide, putting the bulge of his crotch on prominent display in loose, well-worn jeans. It took her a long, lustful moment to recognize Jason. The young man she'd come to know was serious, confident, and respectful. Not someone she'd ever expect to see kneeling in wet earth, half-drunk, and looking like his world had come tumbling down around his ears.

Of course, she'd had to get her mind right and yank it out of the gutter before asking him what the hell he was doing in her garden.

A chime from Sylvie's cell phone interrupted her trip down memory lane. Who was calling her at eleven o'clock at night? She picked up the phone, and almost dropped it.

Her stomach dipped with sudden nerves and she took a couple of deep breaths before answering the video call.

"Jason."

His image appeared on the screen. Propped up against the wooden headboard, he looked relaxed in a white T-shirt and a pair of loose black pants.

"Sorry," he said immediately. "I didn't think you'd be in bed yet."

"I'm not." Why did he think she was? Sylvie reached up to tuck a strand of hair behind her ear and brushed against silken cloth.

Shit. Her bonnet. Blushing, she yanked it off her head. But was him seeing her straightened hair twisted into four sloppy cornrows any better?

She didn't miss the quickly hidden smile on Jason's face. "It's not funny!" Although her own lips started quivering with a smile.

"Come on, it's not like I haven't seen you in a bonnet before."

She rolled her eyes and stuffed the stupid purple bonnet under one of the seat cushions. "What's with the late-night call, sir?"

It felt good to tease him again with a couple of video screens safely between them. Seeing him like this, she could almost pretend this afternoon's make-out session never happened.

"I want to talk to you without you running away again."

"I wasn't running."

Another smile darted across his gorgeous lips.

"Okay, fine. I *was* running, but you have to admit, you did spring something pretty wild on me."

"My dick had a mind of its own this afternoon. I didn't mean for it to come out to play so soon."

"God, Jason! I meant the whole baby business!" She shook her head and he had the decency to look embarrassed.

"Sorry, not sorry?"

"Man, you are learning the wrong American things!" The comfortable rhythm of their banter put her at ease. Laughing at Jason's bashful expression, she left the window seat and climbed into bed, propping up the phone using one of her many thick pillows. Sylvie curled up on her side to keep herself in the camera lens.

His look softened. "There she is."

"What?"

"After this afternoon, I wasn't sure you'd be comfortable with me again. That's why I'm calling you instead of knocking on your room door. I figure our usual means of communication might put you more at ease."

He wasn't wrong.

"Does this mean you're softening me up for something?" Sylvie asked.

Even through the screen, she could see something flare in his eyes. Desire.

An answering heat quivered low in her belly. Sylvie licked her lips and squeezed her thighs together.

"Jason... What are we doing here?"

"I want you to get used to the idea of being with me. Sexually. We should have a baby together and, as comfortable as this is..." He gestured between them. "We can't procreate through a screen."

After spending hours at the café thinking about what Jason wanted and where she stood on the whole baby issue, Sylvie knew one option they had was the infamous turkey baster. But the look on his face said a hollow piece of plastic wasn't what he wanted to plunge deep inside her.

Sylvie's stomach muscles tightened and she swallowed the whimper of want rising up in her throat.

"Can we talk about this more tomorrow?" she asked, despite already knowing what her answer would be. "I promise not to run this time."

Chapter 5

Jason

Jason woke up hungry.

After a night of vivid dreams featuring a naked and orgasmic Sylvie, he miraculously managed not to jerk off before he got out of bed. Showered and determined to follow through with the plans he'd come to Atlanta with, he threw on an old pair of jeans and took his ass to the kitchen. There, at least, he could do something about one of his appetites.

He had a stack of blueberry pancakes already made and was working on the turkey sausages when a noise came from behind him in the kitchen doorway. Jason looked over his shoulder and saw Sylvie with her eyes glued to his ass.

"Good morning," he said, hiding a smile.

Then grinned outright when she jerked her eyes away and pulled on the collar of her yellow blouse. She wanted him. While yesterday's heated kisses had shown him she was attracted to his body, it made him want to howl at the moon with happiness that she couldn't hide it. Not from him, and maybe not from herself. It made what he came here to do so much easier.

He turned back to the stove. "Sit. Breakfast is almost ready."

At a few minutes past seven, sunlight had already cleared the horizon and glowed over the wooden floors and amber marble of the countertops. The kitchen, despite its dark surfaces, blazed with light. Although the time difference between Atlanta and Tarbemi was a big one, Jason wasn't tired. He'd made it a point to wake up early enough to make breakfast and begin his campaign to get Sylvie where he wanted.

In his bed.

Her eyes skated over him again, lingering on his bare chest, his hard stomach, and the V of muscle leading down into his jeans. His belly clenched as if she'd touched him. His dick stirred.

"Um... Let me put some utensils and placemats out," she said. "Do you want juice or water?"

"Both, please."

While he moved around the kitchen, he felt her eyes on his bare back and ass. The sensation of her gaze on him settled a hot ache in his balls and distracted him with micro-fantasies of how Sylvie's hands would feel following the same path her eyes took. His hardening dick poked the range knob.

Maybe he'd made a mistake, coming down to breakfast bare-chested in hopes of visually seducing her. It was working too well. His pants were loose, old, and worn silk-thin in places. Hiding his arousal was nearly impossible.

Once the turkey sausages and scrambled eggs were finished, Jason put all the food on the kitchen island. Sylvie added a bowl of assorted berries, glistening with water, to their mini buffet.

They each claimed a stool and sat down.

"After our talk last night, how did you sleep?" Jason asked.

She blinked at him. "How could I forget about your always direct approach?"

"No idea, wife." He served her before filling his own plate. "Now, stop dodging the question. The person on our video chats is the same person talking to you now."

"Only shirtless." Her mouth quirked up before she reached for her utensils and started to eat.

The kitchen island already wasn't big, but Jason had deliberately put the stools closer before she came down. Their elbows brushed and the smell of Sylvie's body, fresh and sweet from her morning shower, teased him.

"It's too hot to wear a shirt," he said, answering her indirect question. "I'm making myself at home like you always urge me to if I ever came back stateside."

Sylvie nibbled on a strawberry, white teeth sinking into the thick, wet fruit. "And now you're here, wanting a baby."

"No, I'm here wanting *you* to be the mother of my child. Don't make it sound like any woman will do."

She slid him a half-apologetic look. "Okay. I won't."

They ate in silence for a few minutes, knives and forks clicking against plates as they cut into pancakes and sausages, drizzled maple syrup over hearty bites of food, and chewed with pleasure.

"Have you made a decision about our baby?" Jason asked after swallowing a mouthful of berries. "You know what? Don't tell me." He held up a hand as she started to reply. "I haven't had a decent day off in a while. Let's just chill today and revisit this another time."

Was it his imagination, or did she let out a sigh of relief? Maybe she wasn't certain about the decision she'd obviously already made.

"I can get out of your way while you do...whatever." She sipped from her glass of orange juice. "Since you love exploring new restaurants, there are a couple of good ones I can recommend."

"The last thing I want you to do is get out of my way. Remember the bike trail you mentioned a few months ago?" Cycling was one hobby from his youth he hadn't been able to give up. Tarbemi was a country of incredible and varied landscapes, with steep and challenging routes for him to ride. They'd been talking about that when Sylvie mentioned a scenic and lesser-known bike route some friends of hers liked. He was far from the best cyclist in the world, but the adrenaline rush from a fast and calf-burning ride was one of the best things to get his mind off work and put him firmly in his body.

"Of course, I remember. It's actually a pretty good time to go."

"Perfect. Come with me?"

She leaned sideways away from him to give him a firm stare. "You remember I'm not a daredevil rider like you, right?"

"I haven't forgotten anything about you, Sylvie," he said softly, pleased when she lowered her eyes and looked a little flustered. "You love the outdoors. So come out and spend the morning with me." When she hesitated, he played his ace in the hole. "I brought those mini coconut cakes you like from the bakery near my place."

Her eyes widened with interest. "How many?"

"Enough to satisfy even *your* appetite, wife."

A corner of her mouth tilted up and she sucked on the tip of a strawberry she'd swirled in maple syrup. Jason's gut tightened and he barely restrained himself from kissing her.

"Okay then," Sylvie said with mischief in her eyes. "Let's go. *After* you show me a coconut cake."

They left for the bike trail an hour later.

As they rode down the quiet neighborhood street, Jason glanced over at Sylvie. She'd changed into a pale green tank top and matching bike shorts, an outfit that made him furtively adjust his dick. Her long ponytail trailed out of her helmet, fluttering in the breeze as she picked up speed.

God damn. She stole his breath every time he looked at her.

Their tires whispered against the dark pavement while slashes of early sunlight bladed through the trees overhead. Jason drew in a deep breath of the morning air, grateful for the easy silence between him and Sylvie.

As she promised, the scenery they passed was not bad at all. Nothing as incredible as the unspoiled island beauty of Tarbemi, but he admitted to being a little biased where his home country was concerned.

"We can stop here and take a breath," Jason said once they'd climbed up a hill which left Sylvie panting with effort. She was fit, but wasn't used to riding up steep inclines.

"Just a little farther," she panted. "There's a nice lookout point ahead you'll like."

"Okay. I'm following you."

"I like that in a husband." She threw a grin over her shoulder at him and flew down the road.

Soon, they pulled onto a path he would've easily missed. Sylvie got off her bike and he did the same, following her on a small root-choked trail through the trees. Then, the trees mostly disappeared. The path became more rock than dirt with the smooth belly of a mountainside on their left. To their right, a sturdy wooden railing protected them from a steep drop down to a panorama of trees and a narrow river snaking through the multihued green.

They leaned their bikes against the rock face and hung their helmets on the bikes' handlebars. At the railing, Jason drew in a long and appreciative breath. "Look at this..."

The view from the overlook seemed both beautiful and far away, a sea of green trees and blue skies with streaks of pale clouds. A faintly cool breeze brushed his face, bringing with it the smell of the fertile earth and sap from nearby trees. Jason felt like he and Sylvie stood together on the edge of the world.

"Isn't it gorgeous?" Smelling pleasantly of sweat and a hint of her tangerine-scented lotion, Sylvie draped her forearms over the railing and looked down.

"Makes my heart stop." He didn't look away when she caught him staring.

"Jason..."

Did it make him a bad husband that the way she said his name, chiding and fond, made him want to kiss her breathless? She'd probably think so.

"Yes?" He turned his body to face hers.

It was quiet there, with only the sound of far-off birds and the breeze rippling through the trees. Sunlight pleasantly stung his skin.

"What do you really want from me?" A wrinkle settled between Sylvie's eyes.

"Aside from you continuing being my wife and helping me raise our pretty kids?"

Some emotion flickered over her face too quickly to catch. "Don't tease, okay?"

Jason had promised himself not to scare Sylvie off with his naked need. But now, she stood close to him looking more beautiful than in his dreams. Right *here*, within touching distance and not separated from him by too many miles and a video screen.

The gold band on her finger flashed in the sun, reminding him of their brief wedding, and the unwavering way she'd said her vows, not once hesitating to link her life with his. Heat glowed in Jason's chest.

He took Sylvie's left hand in his and threaded their fingers together so their rings touched. "What would you do if I told you I want things to be different between us from now on?"

"You mean you want to have sex?" she asked with the certainty of a woman who had no idea what she was talking about.

"I can have sex with anyone. The person I want is you."

"This isn't fair," she said. But her words were barely a whisper. "What we have works. It's one of the best friendships I've ever had. Don't destroy it because you think there's something better on the other side. What if you're wrong?"

"But what if I'm right?"

Her hand tightened in his but she didn't look away. Something in her eyes said she wanted this thing as much as he did. But he'd never force it on her. Jason took a slow breath.

He'd risked a lot coming to Atlanta. His pride. The valuable friendship he and Sylvie already had. Over the last couple of years, he'd turned away from casual bed partners to focus solely on his desire for another kind of relationship with Sylvie. The mother of his children deserved his fidelity, even if she never asked for it. After getting by with only the company of his own lubed-up fist for months, kissing her yesterday had left him hard and aching and savage with lust. He wanted her. But if she needed time, he would wait.

The strong woman who'd stood by his side since the moment they made the decision to get married five years ago looked up at him with fear in her eyes. Jason's breath caught painfully in his throat. Her fright wrenched something loose in him, making him want to erase his actions of the last twenty-four hours.

He wanted a marriage with her based on what they already had, and also on what they *could* have. Sex. Children. Nights spent together in the same bed. But if she couldn't see herself being in a real marriage with him, he was wasting both their time.

Jason swore under his breath. His hand tightened on Sylvie's. "Never min—"

Her mouth on his smothered the rest of his words. His entire body instantly went hard and hot as her fingers twisted into his shirt and she pressed tighter against him, lifting onto her tiptoes to meet his greater height.

"Kiss me," she demanded against his lips, her sweet breath teasing him.

Sylvie didn't have to tell him twice. His hunger met hers in a devouring kiss that shook him to his toes. A flashfire of need took him and, growling low in his chest, he swept her along for the ride. Jason slicked the delicious depths of her mouth with his tongue, encouraging her desire with a squeeze of her hips, her ass, her thighs. Then she was climbing him, her legs wrapped around his waist, all of her eager weight on him.

The heat of lust rippled down Jason's spine. He swallowed Sylvie's whimpering sound of desire, gripping her tight and backing away from the railing, his blind footsteps taking him toward the boulder where they'd left their bikes. Heat pooled in his balls. His dick was as hard as the rock face scraping the backs of his hands.

He took her mouth in deep, devouring kisses and didn't want to stop, didn't want to let her go. But he also didn't want it to happen like this. Not if she still wasn't sure. He groaned and the sound ripped out of him with the sensation of an animal in pain.

"Sylvie..." He pleaded against her mouth as she leaned back in to nip at his lower lip and dig her nails into his skin through his shirt. "We should stop."

"Why?" Her eyes were passion-clouded but also clearer than they'd been moments ago. "Isn't this what you want?"

"Shit. It is." He panted, trying to think past his desperate need to bury his hard and aching dick into her soft wetness. "I want you so damn much. But you're not sure."

Her hand slid between them and down into his shorts, pulling out his hard length. He gasped when she gripped his throbbing dick. Stroked him. "Don't tell me what I'm sure about, *husband*."

Jason groaned again as her thumb glided over his slit, dipping into the pre-cum already spurting, threatening to buckle his knees. He was trying to be good. He—

"Fucking Christ!"

She moved against his body as she touched him, twisting her waist, and making soft, needy sounds. The intoxicating scent of her arousal wafted up from between her thighs, making his mouth water. She felt like heaven rubbing against him. His entire body trembled. More pre-cum erupted over her magical fingers.

"So you really want this, Sylvie?" He could barely get the words out.

"Fuck me, Jason. Convince me I should have your babies."

"That's not—" He hissed when she pulled back from him and climbed down his body.

He could only stare as she quickly dragged off her clothes and threw them aside. Naked and glistening in the sun, she stood before him. Her body slim with its small breasts, soft belly, and the lush thicket of hair over her mound.

She was the most beautiful woman he'd ever known.

"Please," she said. "I've wanted this for a long time and... you say you want me, too."

He stripped in record time. A quick scan told him the ground was too hard for either of them. But that wasn't going to stop him, not now when she finally admitted she wanted him. He crowded her again and she came eagerly into his arms. *Fuck*, she smelled amazing. Like sweat and lust and the outdoors and all of his fantasies come true.

He claimed her lips again, their lush fullness, her hot tongue. Her breasts were soft in his hands, their weight subtle and their tips hard. He brushed her nipples with his thumbs, gently tugged them as they kissed.

Moaning, she grabbed his hand and put it between her legs. "I want you so much..."

Her pussy was slick and ready for him. Jason groaned at the feel of that sweetness, and let her guide his hand before taking over and sliding two of his much bigger fingers inside her.

When he thumbed her clit, she gasped into his mouth and stumbled back. Reacting quickly despite the lust riding him, he grabbed her before she could slam into the big slab of rock. Jason didn't lose focus. He rubbed her clit in tight circles and soon she was trembling against him, her face buried in his throat as she gasped her pleasure.

"Give me your dick, Jason. *Please.* I want it inside me."

Fuck, he wanted that too. But wasn't sure he'd last more than a couple of strokes.

"I don't want this ride to be over too soon, baby." He thrust his fingers in and out of her wet pussy, scissoring her to prepare her tightness for his size.

Sylvie gasped and writhed on his hand. "If we don't get—get started—" A moan ripped out of her. "—we won't know how it ends." Panting, she took his dick in a firm squeeze that punched a grunt from him.

More pre-cum gushed. Her pussy clenched and ran wet around his fingers. The need thundered in him and suddenly he had to be inside her. He lifted Sylvie again and she put her legs around him.

"Please!" Sylvie leaned back against the rock, her hips tilted up, giving him room to work. Her breasts and belly trembled with her panting breaths. Their gazes met.

In her eyes, he saw a desire that matched his. He saw need. He saw his future.

Jason slid inside her with one smooth stroke.

She cried out. He grunted from the explosive pleasure as heat bolted down his spine. Christ. She was so tight. So incredibly wet.

Jason captured her eyes with his, rolling his hips between her smooth thighs, fucking into her molten heat. Her lashes fluttered in her lust and she licked her wet lips.

His thighs trembled from the exertion. His back worked. His heart soared.

"Harder," she breathed.

Grunting, he sped his thrusts, giving her what she demanded even as his orgasm barreled dangerously close. Not yet. Not yet! The breath heaved in his chest. He braced his thighs wide, muscles burning. Jason took all of her weight, her ass cupped in his palms as he fucked into her, slow and then fast and slow again, sending lightning flashes of sensation through his body. The storm of it gathered in his belly, ready to destroy him with bliss.

The points of Sylvie's fingers digging into his shoulders spurred him on, the slight pain keeping him on the safe side of his orgasm though the fire of it licked at his balls.

His muscles quivered and heat rolled through him. So close...

The sounds of sex, the slap of his flesh against her flesh, filled the quiet overlook. Sylvie clung to him. She gasped and whimpered and moaned his name. They moved together, two heaving waves heading toward the same shore. Her scent overwhelmed him. The pleasure burned.

"Jason!" She cried out his name, her hips a hurricane of movement, her pussy swallowing and squeezing his dick in a maddening, sweat-drenched ride. Orgasm blazed brightly on his horizon. Desperate for her to come, he slid a hand between them and rubbed her clit in tight circles as he hammered into her.

"That's it, love. Come for me."

She gripped his hair and screamed.

Her pussy clenched tight around him as she came, shivering and jerking on his dick. Then he was coming too, emptying his aching balls into her quivering core. Pleasure roared through him, fiery and undeniable.

"Shit..."

Limp with his lungs gasping for breath, Jason braced himself against the boulder, Sylvie sheltered and trembling between his heaving chest and the hard rock face.

Awed by what just happened between them, Jason held Sylvie tight. He was never letting this woman go. She sagged against him, making satisfied sounds and raking her nails along his scalp. The sensation of her fingers in his hair wrung another pulse of pleasure from him.

Suddenly, she stiffened against him. "Do you hear that?"

"No, I don't—" But then he did. The sound of laughter and conversation. People were coming.

Shit.

He winced as she quickly disengaged their bodies and slipped away, scrambling to grab her clothes and yank them on. With his dick and balls flopping around everywhere, he did the same. He didn't live here but he had no desire to be caught butt ass naked in the middle of the woods with his dick wet and the fading flashes of orgasm still lighting up his body.

So much for the afterglow.

With his heart beating faster as the sound of people approaching grew louder, he jerked his shorts on over his shoes and socks, almost landing on his backside.

A snort of amusement pulled his attention from what he should have been doing. Sylvie, much better than him at speed dressing, already had all her clothes on and was moving toward her bike.

"Stop laughing!" But soon he was chuckling too. He pulled on his shirt and jammed on his helmet.

By the time the strangers turned the corner to their formerly private hideaway, both he and Sylvie were fully dressed and walking their bikes toward the path.

"Good morning!" Sylvie smiled brightly at the strangers, two couples covered in sweat and designer riding gear.

"Enjoy the spot," Jason called out to them as he followed his wife.

The four strangers gave them bright but puzzled smiles. As soon as the strangers were out of sight, he and Sylvie looked at each other and burst out laughing.

Chapter 6

Sylvie

"You two look mighty sweaty." Michaela stepped off the front porch as Sylvie and Jason pulled into the driveway on their bikes.

Heat rushed through Sylvie's face at the reminder of what she and Jason had been up to less than an hour ago. As if the drenched state of her underwear wasn't reminder enough. During every moment of the ride back, she'd felt the delicious soreness his thick dick had left behind.

Today, Michaela wore a pale blue bustier and cut-off shorts that left half her ass cheeks hanging out. A different outfit from the afternoon before. The same "steal your man" energy.

"Summertime in Atlanta does tend to make people sweat, Michaela." Jason pedaled ahead of Sylvie and coasted to a stop under the carport. His big thigh muscles stretched the bike shorts and his muscular ass was like one of the juicy peaches Georgia was famous for.

Of course, Michaela was checking him out, too.

Jealousy pricked at Sylvie, but she settled her face into neutral lines as she got off her bike.

Yesterday, she'd been willing to let her sister carry on with her foolishness, but today she wasn't in the mood.

"What's going on, Kayla? You're not usually here this much." Since moving out, Michaela didn't come over very often. The mansion and servants she'd quickly grown accustomed to were more her speed.

Sylvie walked her bike past Jason to the storage shed, not turning around to see if he was enjoying the eyeful of T and A Michaela had brought to the yard.

"I'm here to invite Jason to lunch," Michaela said, raising her voice to follow Sylvie as she unlocked the shed and stored the bike. Her voice lowered, but Sylvie heard every word. "There's a new bistro in Downtown Decatur, Jason. You should come with me. It'll be my treat. I know you missed a lot of the good stuff around here." Her tone made it clear she considered herself the "good stuff."

Sylvie's hand clenched around the shed's door handle as she pulled it closed. When she got back to the front yard, she saw Michaela had drifted closer to Jason. He wore a smile Sylvie hadn't seen in a long time, not since those long-ago days when he'd first come down from Harvard to visit with

Michaela, a stranger with polite manners. It had taken a year of sporadic visits for him to give her a real smile.

"Come on, Jason." Michaela leaned against one of the carport's supporting beams, back arched, one long and bare leg extended like she was showing off the mole on her upper thigh. "Just for old time's sake." He'd apparently refused her offer of lunch. "I promise not to bite."

Who knew the offer of teeth had even been on the table?

Over her sister's head, Jason met her eyes. "Old times are gone, Michaela. There's nothing about them I want to revisit. I'm only here to see my wife. If you want to have lunch with us here at home, and it's okay with Sylvie, we can do that. But I'm not going anywhere with you. That wouldn't be respectful of my marriage."

Sylvie wanted to cheer, but managed to restrain herself.

Michaela put her hands on her hips. Her chin went up. "Where was her respect for *our* relationship when she stole you from me five years ago?"

Stole? What in the revisionist history nonsense was this?

Sylvie couldn't keep quiet. "Kayla, you left him and put him in a bind after you made an agreement."

And when she'd asked her sister—after the fact, but at least she *did* ask—if she'd mind if Sylvie started seeing Jason, Michaela had waved her hand in dismissal, saying Jason had no obligation to her.

Michaela spun around to face her. "I didn't think you'd fucking *marry* him!"

"What was he supposed to do?" Sylvie kept her tone reasonable. "He told you what he wanted from you. You agreed, then took it all back."

"And so you stepped in to be his rescuer? Typical." Michaela sneered. "He doesn't even love you. Not like he loved me."

Sylvie winced. It was only the truth. But it still hurt to hear.

"Michaela, *stop*." Jason's voice was hard. "Why are you acting like this? You don't want me."

Sylvie snorted in disbelief. "She definitely still wants you."

Michaela gave her the finger.

"Then it's too bad I'm not some toy to be thrown aside and picked up again, isn't it?" Jason made an annoyed sound. "When I came back here, I figured I'd have to see you, Michaela, but not like this." He gestured to her, an arm sweeping down to encompass, Sylvie assumed, the revealing bustier and ultra-short shorts and possessive attitude. "You knew what was at stake for me if we broke up. If all you wanted was to have sex with other guys and explore your sexuality, you could have done that."

The shock on Michaela's face was almost funny.

Jason went on. "I remember how young you were. But you turned your back on our agreement and had another man on the side. There's no room in my life for someone who'd do that to me." The muscle in his jaw flexed and something about the expression on his face reminded Sylvie about the hurt boy she'd found grief-drinking champagne in her garden. "So please, Michaela, stop acting as if we're friends." Jason grabbed the bike and turned it toward the storage shed. "Now, if you'll both excuse me, I'm going to take a shower."

"Did you tell him I cheated on him?" Michaela asked after Jason disappeared through the gate to the backyard. Sylvie assumed he would use the "hidden" key and let himself through the back porch.

"No." Sylvie pulled her eyes from the closed gate. "He told me."

"That's a lie!"

Sylvie stepped away from her frowning sister to climb the porch and sit on the bench swing. "Jason mentioned hearing you talk about some other guy's penis on the phone, the same day you broke up with him." Sylvie couldn't remember the name Jason told her, but it wasn't important. The brief flash of guilt on Michaela's face said it all. "It doesn't matter now anyway. Years have gone by. You have kids now."

"They should've been *his* kids," Michaela said.

Logic had apparently flown away from this conversation. "But they're not."

Michaela was quiet as she climbed the porch steps and leaned on the railing near Sylvie. "It's not fair. You weren't ever interested in Jason until I had him."

Sylvie choked out a bitter laugh. "Really? That's what you're going with right now?"

Michaela had enough shame to look away. After all, she'd been the one on a campaign to lure away Sylvie's boyfriends. Not one but two of them had briefly ended up in Michaela's bed while they were still seeing Sylvie. They were guys old enough to know better than to sniff after a teenager. Michaela had only taken them long enough to rub the betrayal in Sylvie's face before moving on to other men.

Sylvie never knew why she did it, and never asked.

It didn't take Michaela long to get over what brief embarrassment she felt. "If you didn't take him to spite me, then why?"

Sylvie shrugged. "Jason asked me to help him."

"*Help.* Right. That's why the two of you just rode up smelling like sex? Because you helped him out?"

Self-conscious heat rushed into Sylvie's face. Still, she rolled her eyes. She wasn't ashamed about having sex with her legal husband.

"After you left Jason, he wasn't your business anymore," she said. "He and I have a relationship separate from whatever you two had." And because the old wound of her sister's cruelty had never fully healed. She continued. "He's obviously done with you, regardless of what you want now."

A sneer curled Michaela's lip. "Better enjoy it because it won't last. You have no idea what it takes to keep a man, much less tempt a husband to stay with you. The outdoor fuck you had with Jason was nothing. He'll always wish I was the one he married."

Sylvie almost laughed. The words stung, but only because Michaela was cruel enough to say them. "If you really believe what you just said then you're still the ignorant child who betrayed a good man for the freedom to make bad decisions."

Michaela flinched, then snarled. "Fuck you."

"I believe that's my husband's job." Sylvie turned her back on her sister and went inside the house.

Chapter 7

Jason

Jason stepped back from the Uber and watched as the black Prius pulled away. Despite the decision he'd made to come here, nerves jangled in his belly. A shrug eased some of the tension from his shoulders as he crossed the parking lot and stepped up to the elegant two-story Craftsman housing Barrington Beauty Bar and its offices.

As he approached the door, he caught an image of himself reflected in the glass. Pale blue button-down, black slacks, his favorite all-black leather Nikes. Casual but obviously a man with business on his mind. The business of his wife.

On Saturday morning, after his shower, he'd come back downstairs to find Sylvie gone. A text message told him she'd left to help a friend with an emergency. Disappointment blindsided him. He'd hoped after what happened between them at the overlook, they could talk about what he was really doing in Atlanta. He never got the chance. She was gone for the rest of the day, and Sunday too. A pre-planned day of brunch and shopping with her girls, she'd said via text.

Now, it was Monday morning and she'd already left the house before he could see her.

She was avoiding him.

He cursed himself for coming on too strong and making love to her during their outing. Despite how they'd left things, she obviously regretted the sex. Maybe leaving her to talk with Michaela alone had been a mistake. His ex was brilliant, able to twist anyone's mind and make them believe whatever she wanted them to. Did she pour some sort of poison in Sylvie's ear?

There was only one way to figure out what was going on with Sylvie. Jason pulled open the door to the beauty bar and stepped inside.

The hum of conversation and the scent of multiple beauty products greeted him as he walked into the brightly lit space. Gold marble floors, soft gray walls, a crystal chandelier overhead that threw sparkles of light on every surface. Although it was barely nine in the morning, the dozen or so beauty stations along one wall were all filled with clients.

Barrington Beauty Bar, formerly Barrington Beauty Supply, felt very elegant and exclusive. Sylvie had done a damn fine job in revitalizing and rebranding the business she inherited.

"Good morning, sir." A woman behind the wide reception desk warmly greeted him. "What can we do for you today?"

He flashed a smile. "I'm here to see my wife. Sylvie."

Curiosity sparked in the woman's eyes and she smiled back at him with every part of her pretty face. "You're Jason!" Her professional mask disappeared and she looked seconds away from clapping in happiness like a kid at Disney. "I've seen your photos. Wow! You're even more handsome in person." A sigh. "Sylvie's in a meeting right now but you can go on back." She waved him toward a door at the rear of the bar. "I'll buzz you in."

Jason thanked her and headed off to find Sylvie.

Behind the door, Barrington's was like a different place. The same gold and gray color scheme reigned here, but with the décor of a professional office rather than a spa. Following the faint sounds of a conversation, he passed through a hallway with several office doors and some unremarkable abstract paintings on the walls.

He ended up at a smoky glass wall, clear enough to reveal two figures inside a conference room. Sylvie and a man he didn't know. Through the slightly open door, he saw a large conference table, a projector, and a podium with a microphone. A meeting seemed to have just ended. Most of the chairs had been pushed back from the table and abandoned coffee cups and pens littered the empty places.

"—said in the meeting, if you're not ready for me to buy you out completely, the partnership offer is very much on the table."

The man, wearing a summer-weight gray suit and looking like a model for men's cologne, stood much too close to

Sylvie. Jason's gut tightened and he forced his feet to stay exactly where they were.

"I don't want a partner, Beau." Sylvie, wearing a soft pink dress and matching heels, neatened a stack of papers before sliding them into her briefcase. "I've told you this quite a few times already. Let this be the last." Her voice was firm.

"You *need* a partner," the man had the balls to say. "What type of marriage do you have if your so-called husband is always gone, leaving you unfulfilled and alone?" He stepped even closer to Sylvie. "You can try to hide the truth all you want, but I can see it. You want to be free of your phantom husband. You want a real marriage with a man who will be by your side. If you and Barrington's were mine, your bed would never be empty and you'd have Barrington Beauty Bar locations all over the United States."

Was that what Sylvie wanted?

"What you *think* I want and what I actually do want are two different things." She snapped her briefcase shut and draped the strap over her shoulder, obviously done with the conversation.

But the man's words ruthlessly pummeled Jason. He'd come from Tarbemi demanding an heir and masking his real motives, but what about Sylvie's own desires? Maybe she didn't want anything to change between them.

"Your husband is never in Atlanta," the guy pressed. "If you didn't want a partner, why get married? If he's there for you like you say, where is he now?"

Jason pushed the door open. "I'm right here."

Sylvie drew in an audible breath.

The fitness model gave him a dismissive look. "An absentee husband *and* an eavesdropper."

"I like to know everything concerning my wife. The methods I use don't matter much to me."

The guy, Beau, sneered and turned to Sylvie. "*Now* your part-time man shows up. Let's see how long he stays this time. Just remember, Sylvie, I'm not going anywhere."

Jason clenched a fist, this close to planting it right in the smug asshole's face. The guy picked up a leather portfolio from the table and stalked out. Once he was gone, Jason pushed the door closed and turned the lock.

"What are you doing here, Jason?" Sylvie asked. She looked annoyed and a little flustered.

"Is what he said true?" Jason jerked his head toward the door the asshole just walked out of.

"Beau said a lot of things just now."

"Do you not want to be married to me anymore?" Jason asked.

Sylvie fiddled with her earring. She abandoned her briefcase on the table and walked halfway across the room. Away from him. "It's complicated, Jason."

"It doesn't have to be." He clenched his jaw and fought to bring up the words she needed. "I never intended for our relationship to be a prison, Sylvie. If you want to, go find a man who'd be better for you."

"I don't want another man." She put her hands on her hips, watching him with an intense look.

"Then what do you want?"

"You want a child." She threw the words at him like an accusation instead of answering his question.

He nodded. "I do." Of course, there was more to it, but the time for that confession had passed.

"Shit..." She turned away, her back stiff under the pink dress. Sylvie shook her head.

That was all Jason needed to know. With his heart wrenching painfully, he backed away. "I'll have divorce papers drawn up. You can be free to marry anyone you want in a couple of months." He unlocked and opened the door. After indulging himself with one last greedy look at Sylvie, he walked out.

Chapter 8

Sylvie

When Jason left the conference room, it felt like he took all the air with him. Sylvie sucked in a deep breath. And then another. But it didn't help. Gasping, she rushed to one of the windows and pushed it open, gulping in the desperately needed air.

Divorce.

No.

That wasn't what she wanted. Saturday, after she'd left Michaela fuming on the front porch, she'd been vibrating with anticipation to talk with Jason about what they'd do next. Where they would live if she had their baby. What other ways would their relationship change. But one of her friends had called with a cheating man emergency and she'd had to leave.

A noise behind her made her freeze up. She didn't turn around. Instead, she squeezed her eyes shut, heart pounding fiercely, and hoped it was Jason.

"Are you okay?"

She sagged with disappointment at the sound of Alicia's voice. Sylvie turned.

Her receptionist stood in the doorway of the conference room with a hand pressed against her chest. "Your husband just left here in a hurry. He looked so... so sad."

Sylvie blinked and straightened. Sad? But he was the one who wanted the divorce. Sylvie took another breath and forced herself to think.

"Did he?"

"Yeah. He was so excited to see you before he came back here." Alicia frowned. "Did Beau do something?"

Beau. The things he'd said. The look on Jason's face as the annoying man made more of a nuisance of himself than usual.

Maybe... maybe there was more to what just happened than Sylvie thought. She sucked in another breath, her hands clenched hard on the window-sill behind her.

"Beau was being his usual self, I think. I need to talk to my husband."

"Okay." Alicia brightened. "You should. Both of you deserve to be happy."

Before she could change her mind, Sylvie grabbed her briefcase and headed for the door. "I'll be gone for the rest of the morning. Call me if there's an emergency."

"Yolanda and I will handle everything here, don't worry."

"Thanks." Sylvie rushed out of the conference room.

Less than twenty minutes later, she was back home.

"Jason!" She called out his name from the front door as she kicked off her shoes. "Are you here?"

Nothing.

Was he already gone? Fear sank into her belly but, holding on to a scant thread of hope, she listened hard for any sounds in the house. But it was eerily quiet.

Jason was a decisive man, something Sylvie had always admired. Once he made a decision, that was it. When they'd agreed to marry, at his insistence, they'd gone to the courthouse the next day.

Now, he'd decided he was finished with their marriage.

Was he already at the airport and on his way back to Tarbemi?

Just as she plucked her phone from her briefcase to call him, it vibrated with a text.

Jason: We should talk.

Sylvie's heart flopped over in her chest. The thought of him giving her one final goodbye before disappearing from her life forever made her feet itch with the urge to run. But no.

She'd hated herself for her cowardly behavior on Friday night. She was an adult, dammit. She didn't run from ugly truths and unpleasant conversations. They'd only find her at the next inconvenient moment, anyway.

Sylvie: Okay. Should I call you now?

Jason: Come to the back porch.

She looked up, frowning. He was still here? Her vulnerable heart acted up again.

Better face this now rather than later. Right?

She stuck her phone in her pocket and went outside, following the steps she'd taken on Friday when she'd unexpectedly found Jason waiting for her. Sweat slicked her palms. Butterflies colonized her stomach. Her heart jumped up into her throat and stayed there.

But when she got to the back porch, it was empty.

"Out here." Jason's deep voice came from the fenced-off garden.

She took the paved path away from the house and under the trellised arbor with its explosion of purple bougainvillea.

The breath stopped in her chest. "What's happening?"

On a blanket spread out on the grass, Jason sat wearing a pair of familiar jeans and a white T-shirt. He stood up and held out his hand.

"Come sit down."

What was he doing? Telling her the terms of the divorce in her own garden? He wouldn't be so cruel, would he?

Despite her apprehension, she took his hand. His fingers felt cold and she gripped them tightly, wanting to warm him up. Sylvie lowered herself to the blanket, still clutching his hand.

"After I left your office," he said, sitting close to her. "It occurred to me, I was a fool."

"About the divorce?"

"About everything." He took both of her hands in his. "Sylvie. I don't want you to have my baby."

She swallowed, the rejection settling in her stomach like acid. But Sylvie tightened her jaw and tried not to show how gutted she was. He didn't want her. Not to be his wife or his baby mama. She flushed hot with humiliation and tried to pull her hands away. He didn't let go.

"I get it," she said. "You don't want to have anything to do with me after the divorce."

His gaze bored into hers and she squirmed against the blanket. "Do you want to divorce me, Sylvie?"

Despite the sadness eating away at her, she narrowed her eyes at him. What kind of question was he asking? "Of course, I don't want a divorce. That's what *you* want."

She tried to pull her hands from his again, and this time he let go. She wished he would just get to the point so she could escape with whatever was left of her pride. Before leaving the office, she'd hoped for...something. But now, not so much.

"Fuck. I think I'm messing this up again." Jason's hand fisted on his thigh and he looked behind him like he was searching for something or someone to help him. "Sylvie, I love you."

"Huh?" She blinked hard at him even as her heart started racing. "What do you...? Huh?"

"I've been in love with you for a while now. Years. I don't just want you to have my baby. I want you to be my wife in every single way. If we have a kid or two, fine. If we don't, that's also fine. My point is, wherever you are, I want to be there too. As a real partner, a lover, not just a friend on the video chat screen."

"Jason, are you playing with me right now?"

"If you don't want the same things, I'd understand." His normally intense expression was even more so. "Fuck, I mean, it would hurt like hell, but I'd respect your decision and be out of your house by the end of the day."

He loved her?

The elation she felt was just too much to contain. Happiness burst under Sylvie's skin and she screamed, launching herself at him. Jason caught her with a grunt, tumbling backward on the blanket with her on top of him. Their lips met, hungry and wet, the slickness of his tongue greeting hers, his hands big and steady on her back.

Shivers of arousal rippled through Sylvie and she wriggled on his lap, pressing down on the hard length there. He groaned and the heat of his hands settled on her ass. They moved leisurely together in a sweet ride Sylvie never wanted to end.

Slowly, Jason pulled back. He was smiling. "Does this mean you want to stay married, too?" He was so beautiful with his adoring eyes that she had to lean in and kiss him again, and again.

"Just try to get rid of me." She kissed him, clasping his face between her hands. "You know what? Don't do that. Just keep loving me. Just like I'll keep loving you."

He surged up to sit on the blanket, nearly bucking Sylvie off in the process. The happiness on his face was as bright as the sun. She laughed, gripping his muscled forearms as he clutched her tight.

"Thank God," he said roughly. Through their clothes, it felt like the pace of his furious heartbeat matched hers. "I hoped you felt the same but wasn't sure."

Sylvie's own hopes had been so modest by comparison. She'd only wished Jason wanted to continue their marriage and they would give their maybe-child a loving home together.

And now, she was getting her wish and more. Sylvie breathed in her husband, his scent of mint and man. All hers.

"I'm absolutely sure that I love you," she said.

Sylvie met Jason's eyes and her heart tripped at the love she saw shining there. The late morning breeze brushed over her bare thighs, making her very aware of how she sat, straddling Jason's lap with her dress shoved nearly up to her waist and his aroused warmth pressed against her hot center. Desire hummed between them, sweet and unhurried.

Jason cleared his throat. "Before we do anything else…

He reached behind him for the basket Sylvie noticed for the first time and pulled out a bottle of champagne along with two glasses.

She laughed, delighted all over again by her husband. "I love a man who comes prepared."

"And I'm definitely prepared to come." He rolled his hips under hers, nudging her clit and making her gasp-laugh. "Later."

Giggling, she leaned away as he popped the cork from the bottle and caught the resulting fountain of champagne in one of the glasses.

"You know, this is the first time I've had champagne since that afternoon you stumbled into me drinking my feelings." A smile tilted Jason's lips as he passed her a full glass.

"What made you decide to drink it today?" The glass was cool between her fingers, the stem delicate.

"You know why."

She did. This day was about new beginnings. Letting go of their old pain and assumptions to find new happiness together. A happiness that included reclaiming what it meant to drink champagne in this garden under a bright summer sky.

"Thank you for making me a happy man, for the last five years and especially now." The dimple flashed in Jason's cheek as he raised his glass. "To our marriage."

Sylvie echoed his words. "And to the sex we're about to have as soon as we finish this toast."

Jason's laughter ignited her own. Then their glasses touched with a clear and bright sound that seemed to echo around the garden, filled with joy.

Thank You!

Thank you so much for reading TO TEMPT A HUSBAND! If you enjoyed it, please take the time to **write a starred review** online – it doesn't have to be a long one – and share your experience with a friend or three.

To keep up with the latest releases and get free reads, subscribe to my newsletter here: https://bit.ly/LindsayEvans

To find me on the web, go to my website www.LindsayEvansWrites.com, Facebook, Twitter, or Instagram pages. You can even contact me by email: LindsayEvansXOX@gmail.com.

On-Air Passion Excerpt

"You should just keep your mouth shut! Nobody wants to hear politics from a ballplayer."

From behind the broad back of his bodyguard, Ahmed moved quickly through the vocal crowd of about two dozen people to get to the doors of the radio station. Some were obviously gawking simply because of who he was—rich, retired at thirty and a consistent presence in the Atlanta club scene and on gossip sites across the internet. Others were there because they smelled a scandal or something close to it. And there were some who were present, like the guy who'd just screamed at Ahmed, because they apparently didn't have anything better to do at ten o'clock on a Wednesday morning.

"Technically you're an *ex*-ballplayer, so you can have opinions on anything you damn well please." Sam, Ahmed's bodyguard and cousin, growled the comment as they slid past the radio station's security guys, just low enough for

Ahmed to hear, although if he'd said it at the top of his voice, nobody would have reacted. Guys over six feet tall with muscles stacked on top of muscles could get away with saying just about anything they wanted to, and to whomever.

Ahmed was built on a more modest but—he liked to think— no less impressive scale with his six and a half feet of lean but defined muscle, a strong jawline and cheekbones that had been accused a time or two of being "chiseled." And those were just the nice things his sisters said about him.

Only the memory of the mellow breakfast he'd had with his family—his sisters, Aisha and Devyn, his mother and Sam— kept his annoyance at the heckler to a low-grade ripple. Besides, the hostility of strangers was nothing new to him, especially after twelve years playing professional basketball. He was now retired and having fun being a part-time radio show host. Even if he'd been silent about his politics, people would still find some way to throw insults his way. Plenty of his former teammates were prime examples of that. The people loved you when you were playing well, making them money, entertaining them. But once you fumbled, good luck.

"Damn, they're rowdy out there today." Sam settled the lines of his dark jacket more firmly on his shoulders with a shrug, the custom-made suit easily hiding his gun and somehow minimizing the size, but not the threat, of his big body. Ahmed didn't know how he could wear it with the crazy-hot January weather currently punishing Atlanta. "What the hell did you do while I was asleep?" His deep voice rumbled in a way that let Ahmed know he was only half joking. Before going their separate ways—Sam to the military and

Ahmed to basketball—Sam was forever pulling Ahmed out of the trouble his big mouth got him into. He'd learned to temper his snarkiness but once Sam got out of the army with an honorable discharge, Sam fell back into the role as body-guard but in a more official capacity.

"You know it's because of that tweet I sent last night," Ahmed said.

"As if the city didn't already know how you felt about it closing that downtown high school." Sam took in the wide and sterile hallway and the half dozen or so people making their way through it with a skilled gaze, taking in details Ahmed took for granted.

"Just making sure they didn't miss my opinion," he said with a scornful twist of his lips.

Marcus Garvey High was a school Ahmed had poured a lot of money and time into to support its STEM program that worked to give city kids an equal chance at tech, engineering and science jobs once they graduated. Although Ahmed had been born into a middle-class family and hadn't faced the challenges many of those kids at the high school did, he knew betting on an elusive sports career or going into the armed forces shouldn't be the only options they saw in their future.

Ahmed was sick of urban kids' education being a low prior-ity. Something had to be done about securing their future. He may not be a politician or even a "real activist," by some standards but he was doing what he could while he had the platform.

"Don't forget we're going to that town hall meeting on Monday morning," Ahmed said.

"Good," Sam said, nodding.

As they made their way toward the studio Ahmed would occupy for the next three hours, Sam walked just behind and to the right of Ahmed, keeping an eye out for whatever possible dangers lurked nearby. Not that Ahmed had stumbled into any hazards after being at the station for his new gig for nearly two months now. The weekly midmorning show was still enjoyable. It gave him a chance to interact with fans—and haters—in a personal way he'd never had the chance to try before. And it was something for him to do after retirement that didn't involve groupies, the successful string of restaurant franchises he'd bought or the various "investment people" he'd had to hire once his money began multiplying even faster than he'd planned.

Sam stepped ahead to push open the door of the studio, and Ahmed moved to step through it when a flash of pink caught his eye, something unusual in his established Wednesday-morning routine. He stopped in his tracks and damn near caught his breath at the vision of femininity floating toward him from down the hallway.

High heels, a pink floral dress swirling around slender legs and hips, a narrow waist he could easily measure with both of his hands. The woman's breasts were small, barely a handful, but like most Black men he socialized with, Ahmed had never been caught up in breast size. Big, small, barely there at all—it didn't matter to him. The rear view was what made him decide whether or not a woman was worth a second look or even a second date.

The Pink Lady sauntered toward him, her hips swaying and high heels loudly kissing the tile floors, making his heart beat faster as she came close. She wore her hair straight and pinned up in some sort of topknot with curly wisps floating around her face.

"Don't swallow your tongue." Sam, still holding the door open, was making a visible effort not to roll his eyes.

Ahmed didn't care. He was already losing himself in a daydream involving thick thighs and a plump backside made for spanking. He had no idea what his Pink Lady was packing in her trunk, but *damn*, he bet it was good. His fingers twitched with the phantom sensation of sinking into her sweet flesh.

Sam pretended to cough into his fist. "Okay, now you're just being a creep."

And he was right. Ahmed couldn't stop himself from just… staring. He didn't want to stop. Above her hips and waist and delicate-looking breasts, the woman's face was *pretty*. Like a daisy in sunlight or a rainbow after a storm, she stunned him with her natural and easy radiance. The image came to him, effortlessly, of tumbling with her into his bed to the music of her laughter and the sweet clasp of her thighs while her thick hair fanned over his pillow.

Damn. She made him want to give up his rule about messing around at work.

But he wasn't a kid anymore. He couldn't afford to be that sloppy about who he took to his bed. Not again.

His—no—*the* Pink Lady was still walking toward Ahmed, but he forced himself to look away from her.

"Let's get in there and do this." He clapped his hands once, a loud gunshot of a noise to get his mind right.

"I'm not the one who needs the pep talk about sticking to business, cousin." Despite his casual words, Sam did his usual thorough scan of the studio's large outer office, only relaxing his stance once he was satisfied nothing lurked in the spacious room to harm Ahmed on his watch.

"Ahmed, my man!" The station's general manager, Clive Ramirez, was a ball of energy. Probably from the four-plus espressos he usually had before lunch.

He stepped out from behind the receptionist's desk, where he had been looking over the young woman's shoulder at something on her computer. With a wide grin, he shook Ahmed's hand. Firm and enthusiastic.

"What's going on, Clive?"

"Life, just life." Short yet muscular, with a belly just beginning to grow from middle age and lack of exercise, Clive Ramirez gave the impression of being a perennially happy man. He loved what he did for a living, fairly treated the people who worked for him, and loved drama like a teenage girl. But everyone had to have a hobby.

Clive followed Ahmed and Sam from the outer offices to the sound booth.

"Nothing wrong with that." Ahmed took off his blazer and draped it over one of the six chairs in the room while Sam stood with his back against the wall, his legs spread, hands clasped easily in front of him as he kept an eye on the single door into the room and the glass partition separating the sound booth from the studio, where the sound engineer and his intern handled their responsibilities.

Over the airwaves, Ahmed could hear DJ Don Juan, who was in the sound booth across the hall, about to wrap up his morning show.

"What's on tap for today?" Ahmed asked Clive. "Anything special or do I just do my thing?" His *thing* was usually to play music, rile up the listeners and entertain them with what his mother called his bee-sting humor. Ahmed would almost do this for free. He settled down into the ergonomic chair with a sigh of bone-deep pleasure then swiveled around to keep Clive in his sights.

The station's GM sat in the chair on the opposite side of the oblong table and its six microphones set up in the center of the soundproof room. "More of the usual," Clive said. "Except we have a Valentine's Day promotion going on. A local woman is supposed to come on with you today to plug her business." He passed Ahmed a sheet of paper. "It's all here. Just introduce her and her business then offer the prize. If it goes well, people will be calling in to win, and she'll get her money's worth in new clients."

"Cool, I can do that." He quickly scanned the paper, noting the type of business, the name of the owner and what she offered. He smirked before he could get his face under control. "Selling romance, huh?"

"What? You got something against selling love? 'Tis the season, my friend."

Ahmed shrugged, not bothering to offer his opinion about romance or love in general. None of the so-called relationships he'd experienced had anything remotely like "love" attached to them. He didn't want to seem like the Grinch or whatever the Valentine's Day equivalent was.

"If you like it, I love it," he said and caught the flicker of amusement on Sam's otherwise stoic face.

Ahmed hid his hand behind his back and shot his cousin the bird. This time, Sam's amusement came with a huff of quiet laughter.

Minutes later, Ahmed eased into the seat, once DJ Don Juan wrapped up his program. He slipped on the headphones and into his on-air persona.

"Hey, Atlanta! It's Ahmed Clark on the air and in your ear for the next—" he looked at his watch, a gift from his father "—two hours and fifty-eight minutes. If you want to talk, call me. If you want to listen, open your ears real wide." And he was off. Grin in place, anticipation for the next few hours bubbling under his skin.

Yeah, he could definitely do this for free.

He fell into the magic of being on air, exchanging laughter and information with his listeners until he got the signal from the sound engineer's intern outside the glass. She flashed him five fingers. Almost time for Gabrielle Marshall to get on the microphone to hawk her goods. He gave Kiara the thumbs-up sign and started to wind down his heated discussion with a listener about citizen responsibility in the digital age. When the woman kept insisting regular people didn't need to share everything they recorded on their cell phones, especially when it came to footage that would inflame the public, Ahmed cut her off with Rihanna's "Desperado."

When Kiara gave him the thirty-second warning, he was ready. The door to the sound booth opened. And it turned out he wasn't prepared.

The Pink Lady from the hallway swept in on a cloud of crisp perfume, like she brought the spirit of autumn in with her, and Ahmed couldn't help but inhale a deep breath of it. The pen he'd been making a note with dropped from his numb fingers and rolled across the notebook, across the desk and then to the floor. He heard Sam snickering. A signal for him to get it together. For real.

But damn, she had dimples. They bracketed her quick smile, and she sank gracefully into the chair across from him to easily fit the headphones over her high swirl of neatly pinned hair. Three diamond studs in varying sizes winked from the lobe of one ear.

"Hi, I'm Gabrielle Marshall," she said. "Most people call me Elle."

Her voice was pure sex. And damn if she wasn't even sweeter looking up close. The smiling lips with just a hint of color. Big Bambi eyes and thick hair he could easily sink his hands into. He forced himself to pay attention to the now instead of the hypothetical future where he had her in his bed. He held out his hand for her to shake.

"Ahmed."

She smiled wider, a curve of glistening and lusciously full lips that made him glad he was sitting down. After releasing her soft hand, he reached under the desk to subtly adjust himself.

Although Sam didn't make another sound, Ahmed could feel his amusement from all the way across the room.

Ahmed cleared his throat and glanced at the timer. "I'll introduce you after this song. You already know what to do, right?"

Why did that sound dirty?

The Pink Lady—Elle—nodded and settled her little purse on the desk. Her lips curved again. The pulse of heat in Ahmed's slacks made him wince. A woman's smile. Really? That was what was getting him hard these days? He must really need to get laid. He could easily picture her being the next woman sprawled, wet and panting, in his bed.

"Here we go," he croaked.

Available Now

A Delicate Affair Excerpt

Golden knew he was in trouble when she walked in.

Brown skin, thick hair, a lioness of a woman striding with a pride of other beauties wearing expensive dresses. They were obviously rich. Young. At least, younger than the crowd that usually ended up at Rosie's juke joint. Younger than Golden's twenty-six. More than half the men in the crowded, smoky dance bar turned to watch the three of them, but he only saw her.

Clive, a guy Golden trusted and who was the reason he had the luck of playing at Rosie's in the first place, jerked his head up from the piano and tilted his head at Golden. The sign for, "What's going on?"

Damn. Ten years, on-and-off, of being friends with Golden apparently gave Clive a clue when Golden's attention veered away from where it should have been.

Golden tipped his head toward the door. Clive, not missing a single key on the piano he played like a madman, looked over at the girls. No way would his friend know which one had made Golden just about swallow his tongue.

"No chance." His friend merely mouthed the words, rolled his eyes, and gave his full attention to the ragtime he pounded out of the piano, placed sideways so Clive could see the audience and rile them up when he stood, shaking out one long leg and then the other, dancing while he played. The music-hungry Saturday night crowd ate it up.

In front of the stage, the sunken dance floor was packed body-to-body. People danced and gyrated and generally had a good-old time while the music played. Marley, the only woman in their band of four, belted out songs about heartbreak and lust while Winston, quiet and quietly intense, tormented the crowd with a rhythm from his pair of tall African drums.

Even though the place was crammed packed to the rafters, Big Ed, the galoot by the front door, hustled over to take care of the giggling girls. He waved them toward a table near the front of the stage and off the side from the dancers. Damn near within touching distance, if Golden got bold enough. He plucked at the strings of his banjo, improvising around Clive's loud and lively rag.

Golden's fingers were sore from playing all night, but he was having too much fun to care. The crowd was jumping and that girl was hot as the fire in his mama's kitchen.

Watching her, he didn't so much as twitch the wrong way. He couldn't mess up the music. Only he—and Clive—knew he was sweating like a hog at the butcher with that fine girl breezing between tables to sit at the big one up front.

Golden knew Rosie, the owner of the juke joint and a notoriously ornery woman, had been saving the main table for her man. But as soon as the girls gestured toward the table with their perfumed and pampered fingers, Rosie gave it up easier than a whore on Saturday night. Those rich girls meant money in her pocket.

Golden had only been in Washington, D.C. for about seven months, but he had already seen what money and power could buy. The only difference up here was that the money and influence was thrown around by Negroes, and people jumped up mighty quick to do whatever these rich Negroes wanted.

The band's latest song wound down to almost nothing and, suddenly, Golden felt everything he'd been too lost in the music to notice before. The sweat running down his face. The rough chafing of the new suit at his wrists every time he moved his hands along the banjo. The hunger that cramped his belly from not eating since his morning shift at Joe's, the restaurant where he worked most days.

Anyone not dancing clapped and jumped to their feet while the rich girls spread themselves around the table, chattering with each other and looking around like they were at a zoo or something. With their bright clothes and brighter laughter, they were like the gems scattered in his mama's jewelry box.

One girl wore red, another green. But the one he couldn't keep his eyes off wore white. Bits of the dress sparkled, and she seemed like a diamond among the others. Expensive and untouchable, cool despite her loud and frequent laughter.

From the way they leaned toward Big Ed and stopped him from walking off, Golden could tell they were demanding drinks. But Big Ed shook his head and gestured back toward the kitchen, where the waitresses were tending to the other customers' drink and food orders. After another emphatic shake of Big Ed's massive noggin, the girls seemed to simmer down. Ed shuffled away as fast as his big body could carry him.

"More! More! More!" The crowd chanted and stomped their feet the way they did every night when the music stopped even for a minute.

The girls settled down and, with a few ringing notes on the piano keys, Clive started up another number. Golden wiped his forehead with the already damp rag he carried in his pocket, stretched his fingers, then poured himself back into the music.

For the length of another set, he managed to forget about the diamond girl and her glittering friends. But at the end of the set, the band scattered. Clive went off to find his girl lurking at the back of the bar, watching for any other woman ready to grab her man. Winston ran to the john to sniff whatever foolishness he had up his nose. Marley, who dressed every day in suits and ties, dipped out the back alley door to grab a smoke. Golden followed.

Instead of standing outside Rosie's back door like the customers did, Golden walked a few yards away to the awning of Swiss Jewel Emporium. The Emporium had been closed nearly a month now. In this neighborhood, it was tough for a high-class place like that, specializing in expensive watches and gems, to survive. Too bad, since Golden had liked the owners, two guys from someplace in Europe. They didn't chase him off when he came in nearly every day to gawk at the cases filled with glittering rings and necklaces. Those pretty things reminded him of his mother and her love of all things shiny.

Golden settled under the Emporium's awning with his back to the rough brick wall and a cigarette in his hand. He stiffened at the sound of footsteps and only relaxed when Marley made herself comfortable just a couple of feet away. He didn't tell her to kick off. As social as she could be, Marley had her own reasons for keeping away from the crowd gathered at Rosie's back door.

Golden was fresh to the city and still trying to get the hang of this smoking thing. Damn near everybody, including Clive, who he'd known back in Opal, said that real city men smoked. Golden didn't see the sense in it, but he had to admit it gave him the excuse to step away from the crowd and sit in his own quiet for a while. He still wasn't used to the rush and noise of the city, of people everywhere and the near-constant clang and clatter of his too-close neighbors. Sometimes, it was just too much. Although he was pushed out of Opal at the threat of a noose for looking at a white girl —which was bull because he preferred his girls as black as his coffee—Golden missed home.

He still longed for those quiet Southern evenings, nights of glow bugs and cicadas and the full moon burning a clear path across a field of peach trees. Seven months and he still yearned for all those things like crazy. But he wasn't returning to Georgia. He had a plan, and it didn't include moving backward.

"I'm heading to the john." Marley tossed her cigarette butt into a nearby puddle. Just before they'd got to the club that night, the rain had come and gone in a flash and left the streets wet but the skies clear.

"All right," Golden said, rolling his still-unlit cig between two fingers. "See you inside."

After Marley took off, Golden tucked the cig into the corner of his mouth and leaned into the bumpy bricks at his back. He loosened his muscles one at a time and breathed out around the cigarette, long and deep.

These days, it seemed to take a lot of work for him to relax.

He'd only just closed his eyes when the sound of raindrops drew him back to the present and into the musty alley. He looked up. From under the protection of the awning, the rain was almost nice. If the idea of walking back to his place in the rain and mud didn't threaten to ruin his one good pair of suit pants, he'd like it more.

Still, it was hard to be mad when a piece of the South visited him in the city like this. Light raindrops falling from the sky, lit by the streetlamps, aglow and surreal.

"That's not how you smoke a cigarette, you know."

The alley wasn't dark, but it was long, just a narrow strip between the building that housed Rosie's and the Emporium on one side and a combination liquor/department store on the other.

A woman walked toward Golden. It seemed like she materialized out of the air. She wore white and floated through the sprinkles of rain with an unlit smoke of her own held between long fingers. The diamond girl.

Golden almost swallowed his cigarette. It was only when he was fumbling to keep it from going down his throat that he heard a flurry of giggling conversation near Rosie's. What the hell? Two other girls stood between him and Rosie's door. They didn't look like they belonged anywhere near an alley. They watched him and Diamond Girl.

She came closer.

"Light me up?" Diamond Girl held the cig under her chin, protecting it from the raindrops sprinkling over her hair and pretty white dress.

The chain from a watch glinted gold against the dress and disappeared into a small pocket at her waist. The sight of her away from the noise and crowd punched him in the chest.

God *damn*, she was pretty.

Fighting breathlessness, Golden fumbled in his pocket for the silver match safe he hadn't yet pulled out for himself. He lit one of the matches with a flick of his fingernail and lifted the flame to the cig already at the girl's dark red lips. She sucked on the white stem of the cig. The tip flared red. In the combined glow from the lit cigarette and the street lamps, her skin looked dangerously soft.

Damn. Just...damn.

No way a woman should be that good looking and not be in a magazine, or a museum.

A smile blossomed on her face, like she knew what he was thinking. Blowing a plume of smoke to the side, she took the glowing cig from her mouth. "That's how you smoke, baby," she said.

He took the one out of his mouth, held it between two fingers, and looked down at it like it had done him some wrong. "It's not really my thing, anyway," he said. "Cigarettes make my mouth taste like ashes."

"Like ashes?" With the burning cig in one hand, elbow bent and balanced in the palm of her other hand, she quirked her moist lips. "What about my mouth, would it taste like ashes, too?"

Shock and a sudden blast of desire shot up Golden's spine. But while his brain was wrecked at the very thought of sipping from her rosy lips, his mouth opened up to save him. "Probably, and it's not a flavor I'm fond of," he said. "No matter where it's coming from."

The quality of the woman's smile changed, becoming less flirty and more flinty, like she'd taken his rejection to taste the cigarette from her mouth personally.

"You're not from around here, are you?" Just like before, she didn't wait for his response. She raised her voice. "Sounds like you just fell off a peach truck fresh from down South."

His fingers tightened around the unlit cigarette. Did this woman just...?

A rush of heat, part humiliation but mostly anger, scorched him from head to toe. Golden knew if they'd been in the bright sun, she would have been able to see every shade of furious red rushing under his pale yellow skin.

Giggles from her friends scurried at him like small spiders.

Golden shoved the match safe in his pocket hard enough to feel a seam break. "I come from somewhere it's considered uncouth and low class to be rude." He looked down at her from his height of just over six feet and realized, even in the midst of his anger, she was only a few inches shorter than he was, the perfect height for kissing.

Snarling at himself, he tucked the limp cigarette behind his ear and stalked toward the entrance of Rosie's, ignoring the pair of brightly dressed girls who gawked at him and giggled some more...

Available Now

After I Do, the series

You're officially invited to attend a month-long celebration of love with twenty seven of your favorite short, steamy romance authors.

They'll make you swoon, laugh, and set your e-reader on fire. These couples will stumble into love, fall for their worst enemy, fight to rekindle lost love, and so much more. Tag along and find out what happens 'After I Do'!

♥ Get the entire series here: https://amzn.to/3sOsKRt

♥ Read the series for free in Kindle Unlimited.

- 2/1 The "I Do" Do-Over by Poppy Parkes https://amzn.to/3JQUTwy
- 2/2 First Blush - Reina Torres https://amzn.to/3hchaZ8
- 2/3 Return of The Mobster - Imani Jay https://amzn.to/36xdpeR

- 2/4 The Marriage Pact - Piper Cook https://amzn.to/3peRhfJ
- 2/5 Wedding Belle - Violet Rae https://amzn.to/354cYbu
- 2/6 The Shadow of Us - Tamrin Banks https://amzn.to/3BO18yg
- 2/8 Wedded Miss - Karla Doyle https://amzn.to/3pekJCx
- 2/9 When We Woke Up - Ember Davis https://amzn.to/3vgI09o
- 2/10 All I Need Is You - Pippa Lux https://amzn.to/3vgSk2Q
- 2/11 Happenstance - Matilda Martel https://amzn.to/3Iis7of
- 2/12 Keeping What's Mine - Carly Keene https://amzn.to/3BPyzjX
- 2/13 More for Us - Allie York-Williams https://amzn.to/3MaCeoL
- 2/14 Cracks in the Windshield - Bree Weeks https://amzn.to/32rh5xg
- 2/15 Mediocre - BF Queen https://amzn.to/3shaNKF
- 2/16 Winning My Wife - Layne Daniels https://amzn.to/3p9Zdif
- 2/17 The Unforeseen Arrangement - Jade Royal https://amzn.to/3hfjZco
- 2/18 Just for You - Haven Rose https://amzn.to/3K9fZqb
- 2/19 Worth the Wait - Silke Campion https://amzn.to/3pd7FgM

- 2/20 Have You Met My Wife? - MK Moore https://amzn.to/350MIZa
- 2/21 More Than Love - JaNese Dixon https://amzn.to/3hg0DXs
- 2/22 Love is All We Got - Kindra White https://amzn.to/3vehNd2
- 2/23 Wearing the King's Ring - Gia Bailey https://amzn.to/35rqw0M
- 2/24 Pre-Arranged Love - Andrea Marie https://amzn.to/3Il82gO
- 2/25 No Ordinary Love Story - Kelsie Calloway https://amzn.to/3M9vnVg
- 2/26 Run Away with Me - Macy Fox https://amzn.to/33Ok97h
- 2/27 The Biker Takes a Bride - Jailaa West https://amzn.to/3hbHsen
- 2/28 To Tempt a Husband - Lindsay Evans https://amzn.to/3ACvFge

Also by Lindsay Evans

Novels Available Now

Affair of Pleasure

Bare Pleasures (Miami Strong)

The CEO's Dilemma

A Delicate Affair

On-Air Passion (The Clarks of Atlanta)

Pleasure Under the Sun

Snowy Mountain Nights

Sultry Pleasure: A Billionaire Romance

The Pleasure of His Company (Miami Strong)

Untamed Love

The Wrong Fiancé

Professional Lovers Series

Seducing the Stripper (Professional Lovers Series Book 1)

Novella Anthology

Dim the Lights

About the Author

Born in Jamaica, Lindsay Evans currently lives and writes in Madrid, Spain. A writer of sensual love stories, she loves good food and romance and would happily travel to the ends of the earth for both. Find out more at www.LindsayEvans-Writes.com.